To my sister, Linda Catherine –PH

For those who dare to try –JB

Tundra Books, an imprint of Penguin Random House Canada Young Readers,
a division of Penguin Random House of Canada Limited

Library and Archives Canada Cataloguing in Publication

Title: Out into the big wide lake / Paul Harbridge ; illustrated by Josée Bisaillon.
Names: Harbridge, Paul, author. | Bisaillon, Josée, illustrator.
Identifiers: Canadiana (print) 20200215914 | Canadiana (ebook) 20200215922 |
ISBN 9780735265592 (hardcover) | ISBN 9780735265608 (EPUB)
Classification: LCC PS8615.A678 O98 2021 | DDC jC813/.6—dc23

Published simultaneously in the United States of America by Tundra Books
of Northern New York, an imprint of Penguin Random House Canada Young
Readers, a division of Penguin Random House of Canada Limited

Library of Congress Control Number: 2020936840

Edited by Samantha Swenson
Designed by John Martz
The artwork in this book was rendered in mixed media.
The text was set in Iowan Old Style.

Printed and bound in China

www.penguinrandomhouse.ca

1 2 3 4 5   25 24 23 22 21

Penguin
Random House
TUNDRA BOOKS

The brave, loving girl in this story was inspired by my brave, loving little sister Linda Catherine Harbridge. Linda, who has Down syndrome, has lived her whole life in Gravenhurst, Ontario.

Linda was an excellent athlete and won a medal in swimming for Team Canada at the Special Olympics in Vancouver. She played baseball and golf and won $1000 in a bowling tournament. She went on long bike rides and once came face-to-face with a black bear! She still loves swimming and has just taken up snowshoeing.

Parbuckle was based on our family's black-and-white dog Benjie. Linda and Benjie did everything together and often went boating with my father out into big wide Lake Muskoka.

—Paul Harbridge

Out Into the
Big Wide Lake

Written by Paul Harbridge • Illustrated by Josée Bisaillon

tundra

A stick with an arm and a leg. That was a 'K.'
'A' was a tent.
Be careful. Stay between the lines.
'T' was a telephone pole, and 'E' was a little comb.
Her name was Linda Catherine but everyone called her KATE.

There was a knock, knock, knock at the door.

Kate wasn't supposed to answer it — even though she was big now.

The door opened. A woman stood on the porch.

"Hello, Pumpkin," said the woman.

"Grandma!" cried Kate, and ran to give her a hug.

"Grandma wants you to go and stay with her and Grandpa for the summer," said Mom.

"Me?" said Kate.

"Why not?" said Grandma.

"Kate has never done anything like that," said Mom nervously.

"You did when you were her age," said Grandma.

"I know," said Mom. "But Kate . . ."

"Give her a chance," said Grandma.

Next day, Grandma and Kate got onto a smoky train. It was a shaky trip with lots of clacking and whistles blowing. The train chugged past farms with cows and over rivers and through forests, and Kate waved at three deer standing on a hill.

After a long time they came to a big blue lake, and the train squealed and stopped with a jerk.

Grandpa waved at them from the platform. He hugged Kate, and a black and white dog named Parbuckle licked her face.

Grandpa helped her into a little wooden boat that moved side to side, forward and back — sort of like a swing. Grandma pulled a cord, a motor started, and away they went.

Puck, puck, puck! Out into the big wide lake.

The setting sun reflected pink on the dark water. Kate felt cool spray on her face that smelled like fish.

They stepped out onto a dock that wiggled under Kate's feet. They went through a store — her grandparents' store — to their home at the back. They ate beef stew and apple pie and watched the sun go down, and Kate helped Grandma build a model boat.

Then it was time to sleep. The bed was strange. Grandma said it was Mom's bed when she was little. Somewhere outside, far down the lake, a bird called. It sounded sad and lonely. Kate wished she were home.

Next morning, after sweet tea and pancakes and
sticky syrup, Kate helped Grandpa carry groceries
to the boat. When it was full, Grandpa threw off
the ropes and started the engine.

"All aboard!" cried Grandpa.

"Me?" said Kate.

"Why not?" said Grandpa.

Kate waved at two men fishing and at a boy and a girl in a
rowboat. Grandpa took the boat into a dock and handed bags of
food to a woman in an apron.

"Who's this?" said Mrs. Wellington.

"My granddaughter, Kate. She's going to be my first mate this
summer."

"I'm sure she'll be a big help," said Mrs. Wellington.

They stopped at more docks, and Grandpa and Kate handed out
bags and boxes.

"Good morning, Mrs. Domanico."

"Fine day, Dr. Chan."

"How are you, Mrs. McKenzie?"

"One more stop and then home for lunch," promised Grandpa.

They came to a part of the lake with big rocks
on both sides. Grandpa took the boat in slow
and careful.

They made it through and came to a dock.
The dock was old and broken, and a thin man
sat waiting.

"Good morning, Walter," said Grandpa.

"You're late!" said the man. He sounded mad. He looked mad, too.

Grandpa passed the man a box, and the man kneeled down and looked everything over. He counted the potatoes and smelled the milk and poked a long finger through the string beans.

"Bruise on this apple," he said. "The girl must have dropped it."

"She did not," said Grandpa.

After lunch, Grandpa worked in the store. Grandma was down at the dock, pouring gas into the outboard motor of the little wooden boat.

"Jump in," said Grandma to Kate and Parbuckle.

Grandma pulled the cord, and the motor started up. Off they went. Puck, puck, puck! Out into the middle of the bay.

"Come sit beside me," said Grandma.
     "Me?" said Kate.
     "Why not?" said Grandma.

Grandma took Kate's hand, and they steered the boat together. Pull, and the boat went one way. Push, and the boat went the other.

Grandma took her hand off. Kate steered the boat in a circle.

"A natural sailor," said Grandma.

Every day, Kate helped Grandpa deliver groceries.

Kate liked everybody and everybody liked her. All except that old man Walter.

In the evening, Kate and Grandma went out in the little boat. The steering was tricky, but Kate finally figured it out. She learned to bring the boat in easy and tie her up using a special knot.

Grandma showed her how to cut into waves so the boat wouldn't tip. One windy evening, the waves were high, and Kate got mixed up and turned the wrong way. That was scary. The boat rocked so hard Parbuckle fell out!

It was morning, near the end of summer. All the groceries were down
on the dock.

"Oh!" said Grandpa suddenly.

He touched his chest and sat down hard on the bench. Parbuckle
began to whine.

Kate ran and got Grandma. A neighbor drove her grandparents to
the doctor. Kate and Parbuckle stayed behind.

The lake was very quiet. Kate and Parbuckle sat on the bench.

Kate looked at the groceries. She thought of the people. She looked at the little boat.

Parbuckle looked at Kate. He seemed to say, "Who's going to deliver all this food?"

"Me?" said Kate.

"Why not?" said Parbuckle.

Soon the groceries were on board. Kate untied the ropes.
She pulled the cord. Off they went. Puck, puck, puck!
Out into the big wide lake.

Mrs. Wellington was surprised to see them.

"Where's your grandfather?" she said.

"Sick," said Kate.

"Oh dear," said Mrs. Wellington.

Then Kate and Parbuckle surprised Mrs. Domanico,
Mr. Chan and Mrs. McKenzie, too.

Kate looked at the last box.

The word on the side said 'Walter.'

Kate looked at Parbuckle. She wanted to go home. Then she thought of the old man sitting there, waiting and waiting.

Off they went. Puck, puck, puck!

The little boat came to the part of the lake with big rocks on both sides. Kate went in slow and careful. Parbuckle looked nervously into the water.

The man was on the dock.

"You?" said Walter. "All by yourself?"

"Yep," said Kate.

Kate handed him the box. Walter knelt down to sort through the groceries.

"Where is your grandfather?"

"Sick," said Kate. She touched her chest.

"What?" said Walter. He stood up with difficulty and slowly stepped down into the boat.

Kate looked at Parbuckle.

"Get moving!" said Walter.

Kate pulled the cord and took them back out. Puck, puck, puck!

"Faster!" yelled Walter. But the little boat was going as fast as she could.

A wind came up and big waves appeared. The little boat started to rock. A wave came over the side and soaked them.

Kate turned the boat into the waves like Grandma had shown her.

The little boat was working very hard, going up and down the big dark waves. Finally they reached Grandpa's dock.

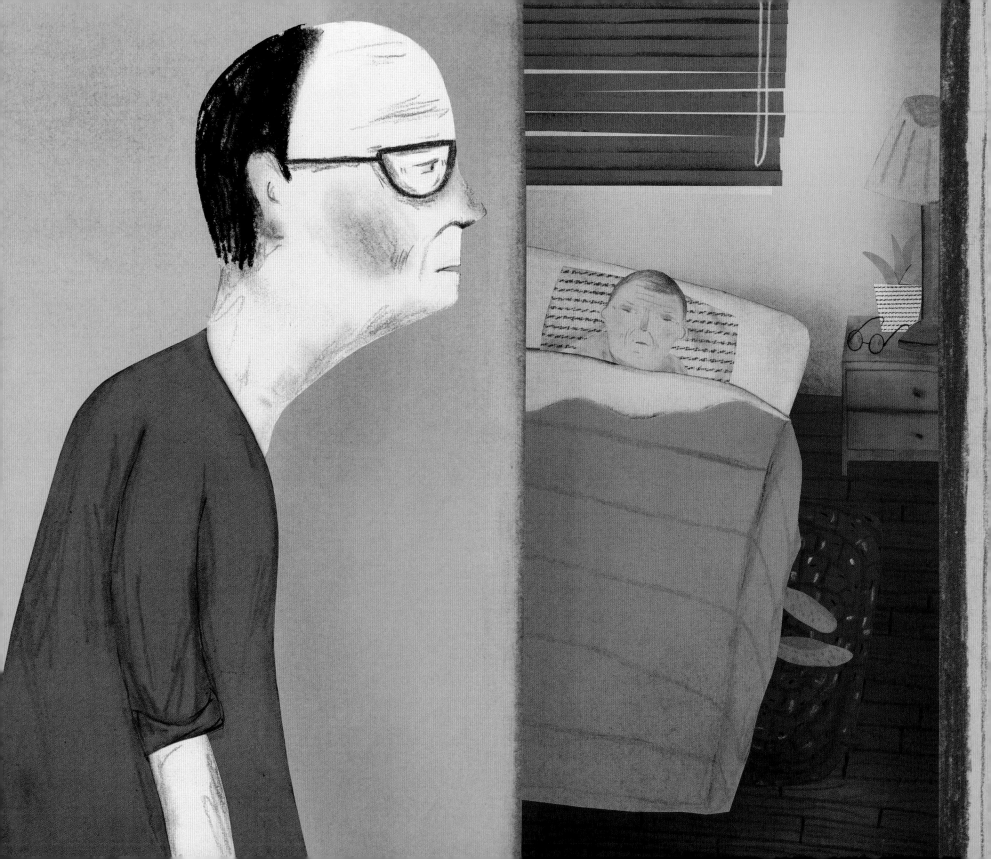

Grandpa was asleep in bed.

"He'll be fine," said the doctor. "But he can't work for several days."

"Thanks for coming to see your brother, Walter," said Grandma when the doctor went out. "He'll be happy to see you."

Walter was Grandpa's brother? Kate couldn't believe it!

Mom came on the train the next day. For two weeks, she and
Kate made Grandpa's deliveries.

"Just like when I was a girl," said Mom.

Summer was over. It was time for Mom and Kate to go home. Grandma, Grandpa and Parbuckle went with them to the station. So did Walter.

Parbuckle licked Kate's face, Walter shook her hand and Grandpa gave her a hug.

"I knew you could do it, Pumpkin," said Grandma. She kissed Kate on the top of the head and gave her a box tied with string.

Mom and Kate found their seats. The train started to move. Kate waved. The people got smaller and smaller and then she couldn't see them anymore.

Kate opened the box. Inside was a little wooden boat. A black
and white dog sat at the front. At the back there was a girl.

"Who is that brave girl?" said Mom.

"Me!" said Kate.

"Sure is!" said Mom, and gave Kate a great big hug.